D0466199

HELLO NINJA

By N. D. Wilson Illustrated by Forrest Dickison

HARPER
An Imprint of HarperCollins*Publishers*

Hello, ninja.

Yes, hello.

What do ninjas do all day?

Ninjas hop.

Ninjas Chop.

Ninjas love to belly flop.

Ninjas scamper here . . .

and there.

Ninjas love to cut your hair.

Ninjas dance.
Ninjas prance.

Ninjas train the king of France.

Ninjas pose up on their toes

every time a blizzard blows.

The bravest ninja finds a foe

to help his ninja legend grow.

A messenger who knows kung fu.

A sneaky thief who's hungry too.

Ninjas dodge and ninjas spin

and show those foes how ninjas win.

They never break; they barely bend.

But even ninja days must end.

And when a ninja's sent to bed,
he saddles up a dragon's head

and flies away into the night,
to chop and dance until it's light.

Hello, ninja.

Shh, not yet!

Ninjas ninja hard all day.
They need to sleep before they play.